FLASHBACK

SHARP SHADES 2.0

FLASHBACK

John Townsend

Ransom

SHARP SHADES 2.0
Flashback
by John Townsend

Published by Ransom Publishing Ltd.
Unit 7, Brocklands Farm, West Meon, Hampshire GU32 1JN, UK
www.ransom.co.uk

ISBN   978 178127 992 2
First published in 2016

CONTENTS

ONE

I could never sleep. I'd wake each night crying. Yelling.

The nightmare came every night. It was always the same. I'd see a face lit by the moon. Staring eyes.

I'd feel breath on my face, and a hand like a claw at my throat. I'd hear the axe fall. Then a spray of blood … and the gunshot.

That nightmare started when I was a boy. Flashbacks smashed into my dreams after I did a terrible thing – in the war.

I'm an old man now. After all, the war ended over 70 years ago. I've lived with a dark secret all that time. I've never been able to tell the truth before.

Until now.

Not long ago I went back to where

it all happened. I had to bury my demons. I had to destroy the nightmare forever. I couldn't risk taking the secret to my grave. It had to be buried alone – once and for all – in the right place.

The simple truth is this: when I was thirteen I killed someone. I didn't go to prison for it. My punishment was a lifetime of nightmares. That's because I've never been able to forgive myself.

If only I could put back the clock. Not a day goes by when I don't think about what I did and I say those two words over and over again: *if only*.

If only it had been different. If only I wasn't a killer.

If only I could go back …

TWO

I was ten when the war started. A year later bombs fell in our street. I was sent away to be safe in the countryside.

I went by train with the rest of my

school. We had to wait in a village hall for people to take us to live with them.

No one chose me, so I was taken to Home Farm. It was an old damp house, run by the dreadful Bensons. They didn't want me, but they had no choice.

Farmer Benson's first words to me were, 'There's no food here for you. There's a war on. Blame Hitler if you starve. We don't get much money to feed you. We hate children as much as we hate Germans. If you wet the bed, I'll rub your nose in it and beat you.

We have rules here, so make sure you keep them.'

Mrs Benson was no better. She stared at me with cold, piggy eyes. In fact, she looked just like the pigs on the farm. Their son, Norman, had pigs' manners, too. He was a few years older than me and would grunt before hitting me for no reason.

I tried to keep away from the Bensons and stay in my cold bedroom above the pig yard. I got very homesick and cried myself to sleep. I wasn't allowed a candle, so it was always dark and scary in my room.

I was glad to go to the village school where I could get away from Home Farm. My new teacher was Mr Green and he was wonderful. We got on well and he was always kind.

'I tried to teach Norman,' he said. 'I know what Home Farm is like. If we had room at the schoolhouse, you could live with us. We've already got four evacuees. But you can still come to tea with us.'

Mr Green's wife had died and his son was away in the R.A.F. His daughter was sixteen and lived at home. She was Julia and was

training to be a nurse. She had a
heart of gold and I adored her. How
different from the Bensons!

Every night Mr Benson swore about
the air raids. A nearby town got a
direct hit. We all hated the
Germans. I hated the Bensons
almost as much.

But at least I had hope. I had
Mr Green and Julia as my friends.

THREE

We often heard planes go over the farm at night. Norman would run out and swear at them – even if they were the R.A.F!

Julia was the only person who

didn't hate the enemy. 'They're just like us,' she said. 'A few bad ones make trouble, that's all.'

That wasn't what the Bensons said. They swore all the time about the war. I was glad they kept so busy and left me alone.

I played in an orchard at the back of the farm. It was overgrown and no one ever went there. At the far end I found an old henhouse that hadn't been used for years. It was covered in ivy, but was a good place to make a den. I'd use it as a secret hide-out to escape from the Germans and the Bensons.

I sneaked into barns to find things to use in my den. A wooden box made a good chair and an oil drum made a table. With sacks and a blanket on the floor, it became my own cosy den. I could be safe and alone with my books – and candles that I took from the kitchen.

The Bensons didn't seem to care where I was, so long as I didn't bother them. They said they needed extra help on the farm, but I was a feeble 'townie', so I was no good. A farm in the next village used Germans to work in the fields. They came from a nearby prisoner-of-war camp. Norman said he'd rather work twice as hard than have a German near Home Farm.

'I'll blast their brains if they come here,' he said. 'They're even worse than slum kids like you.'

There were eels in a stream at the end of the orchard. I scooped one into a bucket and took it back to my den.

I had no idea what I was going to do with it, but I sat inside to admire my catch. I was busy humming and peering into the bucket when I heard a noise. I looked behind me and saw a hand move behind the oil drum. Someone had broken in.

FOUR

A face with grey eyes blinked up at me.

'What are you doing here?' I snapped.

The face tried to smile. 'You have

a good eel there,' he said. 'Did you just catch him?'

The man added slowly, 'You must be a good fisherman.'

'But what are you doing here?'

He replied, 'Don't worry. I am your friend.'

'How can you be? Who said so? I don't even know you.'

I began to panic in case he was a friend of the Bensons.

'Do you know Mr Benson? You won't tell him about my den, will you?'

He closed his eyes. 'I won't tell a soul.' He made a sort of hiss.

'Is something wrong?' I asked.

'I am hurt.'

I could tell he was in pain. I lit a candle and crawled over to him. His knee was torn open and there was a lot of blood.

'You've got a nasty gash,' I said. 'What happened?'

He looked at me for a long time. 'Can I trust you? If you help me, I will tell you a secret.'

I thought of Julia. I was sure she'd want me to help him.

'All right,' I said. 'I'll help you.'

He tried to sit up. 'If I can stay in your nice shed, I will tell you my

secret. But can you bring me a
bandage and hot water?'

I smiled. 'No one will be in the
kitchen right now, so I won't be
long.'

I ran back to the house. The
kitchen was empty, so I took an
apple, a potato, a glass of milk and
a first aid box. There was an old oil
stove in one of the sheds so I took
that, too. It would heat my den and
I could cook something on it for my
guest.

'Do you like fish and chips?'
I asked. I chopped the potato in a
pan.

'That sounds good,' my visitor said.

I looked into the bucket at the eel. 'Well, *sort of* fish.'

I did my best to wash the man's knee. It was in a bad way.

'Thank you,' he said at last. 'You are a good doctor as well as a good fisherman. Those chips make me think you are a good chef, too.'

It was great to know I was doing a good job. The food cooked on the stove and the den filled with fumes. I felt proud of myself for once.

That night, Mrs Benson slopped stew on my plate.

'Not for me, thank you. I'm not hungry,' I said. I was still full from eel and chips.

'Good. I'll have it.' Norman took my plate away.

As the Bensons slurped their stew, they swore more than ever. They were all in a bad mood. Norman told me I could be killed in the night. What he said next gave me a real shock. I now knew I was in the middle of something very scary – right up to my neck.

FIVE

Mrs Benson held tweezers as she bent over her husband.

'Careful, woman,' he screamed. 'Blast the blackout. Blast the Germans. Blast my head!'

His head was full of thorns. He'd been out in the dark, hunting for a German in the woods.

I asked Norman what was going on.

'Don't you know nothing, you thick head? Don't you know there's a German on the run? He got out the prison camp. If I see him, he's dead. He won't last long out there. It'll freeze tonight.'

They said the German had been bitten by a guard dog as he climbed the fence.

'The police and home guard will soon hunt him down. He can't lie low for long. No one would dare give him a bed or food. If they did, it's a crime. If I hear of anyone helping a German, I'll shoot them myself. I keep a loaded shotgun under the bed, just in case.'

Mrs Benson chipped in, 'If a Jerry comes in the night, I've got a knitting needle under my pillow. I'll stab his windpipe.'

So now I knew. The man out there in my den was the enemy – a German. I'd already helped him and it was a crime. I could be locked up for that. Away from Julia and Mr Green.

If the Bensons knew I'd given their milk to a German, they'd beat me.

I'd have to keep it secret.

As soon as they went to bed, I crept from my bedroom. I took a blanket from a spare room and tiptoed down to the kitchen. I'd seen Mrs Benson take a secret swig of brandy from a bottle in the pantry. I poured some into a cup, cut a chunk of bread and went out into the yard. The dogs barked as I ran to the frosty orchard.

The sky was lit by a spray of stars

and a thin silver moon. As the door to my den creaked open, the oil stove hissed. It was warm and cosy inside. The man in the corner sat up with a start.

'Ah – thank God it's you.' His English was good, but now I could hear he was German. I gave him the blanket, bread and brandy.

'I know who you are,' I said.

He looked at me with worried grey eyes.

'But you are keeping it a secret?'

'Why do you think that?'

He pulled the blanket around him. 'Because you help me. You

bring me more things and I can tell you are a kind boy.'

It felt odd to be talking to the enemy. But I liked him. He made me feel important.

'You must not get in trouble for me,' he said. 'Don't take risks.'

I told him it was too late now.

The bandage on his knee had stopped the bleeding. He couldn't bend his leg and I could tell he was in a lot of pain.

'It was a dog, wasn't it?' I said. 'They'll be out with more dogs when it's light.'

He looked worried. 'I came down the stream so dogs would lose my scent. Am I safe to stay in here?'

'Of course. No one comes down here. You are the first.'

I looked at the pain in his young face. I knew then that I was being brave for the first time in my life. It felt good. I'd made up my mind to help someone. Never mind the risk. There was no going back now.

SIX

The next morning, I crept into the
chicken house. I took an egg from
under a hen and ran to my den.

'I can tell you are a good friend to
me,' the German said.

As I cooked his egg, he told me his name was Franz. He was twenty and came from Berlin. He showed me a photo of his sister, who was my age. He told me how he missed her and I even felt sorry for him.

Later at school I heard gunshots from the woods. Everyone was talking about the German on the run. We had to keep doors locked at all times.

After school I ran back to the farm. No one was about, so I took bread from the kitchen and ran to my den.

Franz lay in the corner but he didn't move.

'Are you all right?' I asked.

He just stared. Something was wrong. 'I have a fever,' he mumbled. He was shaking and sweating. Then he groaned words in German.

I looked at his leg. It was in a real mess. He'd been sick and I began to panic. He needed a doctor and I knew I had to get help fast. I'd have to find Julia. She'd know what to do – she was a nurse.

I ran as fast as I could back to the schoolhouse. Julia said she'd come with me to help my friend. 'Tell me what the matter is, Bernard. Who is it and what's wrong? Why are you so upset?'

She got her bag and I led her to the den. On the way I told her the whole story. At first she said nothing.

'You will help us and make him better, won't you?' I said.

'I'll do what I can, but I'll have to report it. You've done a brave thing, Bernard. I'm proud of you.'

We got to the den as Franz was being sick again. He didn't seem to know me or where he was. His leg was wet and smelly. Julia said she'd have to sew up the skin on his knee and splint his leg. He'd need washing and a lot of nursing.

In the kitchen that night, the Bensons asked me tricky questions.

'Where do you spend all your time, boy? You're eating too much these days. There's never any bread or eggs.'

Norman said the police had set up roadblocks to catch the German.

'He won't get far. They'll soon shoot him – and any fool who'd help him. I reckon he's lying low. They'll soon flush him out.'

I said nothing.

Franz was very ill for a week. Julia spent all her time with him. She looked tired as she gave him milk from a cup.

'I think we're over the worst,' she said. 'Franz is going to be all right.'

He could now sit up on his own.

'You have both been very kind,' he said. 'You have saved my life.'

Julia's look said it all. She knew our worries were far from over. What could we do with a German on the run in the middle of England?

I was so glad Julia had helped us. I was also glad she liked Franz. It was great to know they were now good friends.

SEVEN

The weeks flew by. When snow fell,
I had to keep away from the den.
My footprints would give away my
secret.

Franz grew stronger and at last he

could walk on his bad leg. Julia went to see him most days.

One night, we all sat in my warm den as the rain beat down on the roof. We ate the last of the pears I'd found in a barn. Franz held a pear pip and said, 'I shall bury this in the earth. One day a pear tree might grow here among the apple trees. Like me, a stranger. We shall come here when the war is over and sit under my pear tree.'

The hunt for Franz had moved on. The police were looking for him at the coast. Even so, Mr Benson still kept his shotgun under the bed.

On a clear spring night I sat with Franz in the orchard under the stars. He said, 'I look at the moon and think of home. Right now it's shining down on my house in Germany. My family will look up and see this same moon. If only I could be with them.'

He gave me a letter. 'If I don't make it … will you get this to my family? Their name and address are on it.'

'Don't say that,' I said. 'You'll get back one day. We'll keep you safe.'

He put his hand on my arm. 'You

have been a real friend to me, Bernard. I can never thank you for what you have done. I want you to have this – to keep always. I wish I could give you more.'

He gave me his watch, then slid a ring off his finger. 'I want you to give this to Julia if I get taken away or hurt, or … This is all I can give her.'

I told him not to talk about getting hurt. It upset me to think about it.

'I'm very fond of Julia,' he said.

'Yes, I know. So am I,' I said. I had no idea what he really meant.

A few nights later, the three of us played cards in the den. It was my thirteenth birthday and my mother had sent me a little box camera. The next day I took photos of Franz and Julia in the orchard. The war seemed to melt away and we forgot about the bombs. We even spoke about what we'd do when the war ended.

A week later, Franz and I raced paper planes down the orchard.

'My Spitfire will go further than your feeble German Heinkel,' I laughed.

My plane soared from the den, but Franz snapped, 'Get down! Someone's coming.'

I peered through a gap in the door. It was Norman with a shotgun.

A sudden bang shook the den. I saw Norman pick up a dead rabbit and carry it back to the house.

'That was close,' Franz sighed. 'Too close.'

What he said next upset me.

'It's not safe here now. It's time for me to go.'

EIGHT

Julia and Franz had made plans.

'It's not safe for me to stay here any longer,' Franz said. 'I must get back home. My family needs me. I don't want to leave you, but it's for the best.'

'But you'll never get back to Germany on your own,' I sobbed.

They told me their plan. Julia was going to cycle with him to her cousin on the Isle of Wight. From there, Franz would steal a boat and row to France, where he'd be safe.

I was upset. I didn't want him to go, but I also felt left out. They were going without me. They didn't need me now.

I made my own plan to cook a big meal. But as I sneaked into the pantry, Norman was waiting.

'Oi, kid. What are you doing?'

'Er – just a bit hungry, that's all.'

'Get your hands out of there. There's a war on. *Workers* need food, not you weedy brats. What are you taking? I bet it's you who took the axe from the wood shed. I'll have to keep a closer eye on you.'

I said it wasn't me. But I hadn't put it back after I'd chopped wood for a campfire in the orchard. I'd have to take more care.

Franz was to leave on Sunday morning. It was the one day when the Bensons were out of the way. They always went for breakfast with Mr Benson's mother. That would give me chance to use the kitchen to cook Franz a good meal to send him on his way.

I got a tray, plates, toast, butter, jam, a pot of tea, eggs and a vase of flowers. Franz would be so pleased and tell Julia what a clever chef I was.

When I got to the den, I opened the door with 'Good morning, Franz.'

The door slammed in my face. The tray crashed at my feet. Hot tea sprayed over my bare legs. Plates smashed and the flowers fell in the mud. I yelled in horror – not just from the mess and my burning legs. It was what I saw. They were both in the den. Julia was with him. They were lying together.

Franz shouted at me, 'Go away. Leave us alone.'

I heard Julia's voice. 'He doesn't understand.'

I felt sick – and full of rage. How dare they do this to me. He'd taken her away from me.

I'd seen enough. I ran back to the house. I'd show him. I'd make him think twice. I'd make him say sorry.

The Bensons' old truck turned into the yard. That wouldn't stop me now. I went into their bedroom and grabbed the shotgun under the bed. I'd show them I wasn't a stupid little kid. I'd make them all think again.

I stormed back to the den. The rest happened so quickly. I didn't mean to do it. Franz came towards me through the orchard. He had fear in his eyes when he saw how mad I was. He put up his right hand and held an axe in his left.

A loud shot rang out and the gun kicked me in the chest. Birds flew from the trees and then deathly silence.

I blinked through the smoke to see

Franz lying flat on his back. Blood bubbled from his mouth. The axe fell with a thud. His grey eyes were open – staring up at me. He didn't move.

The only sound was my cry: 'What have I done?'

NINE

Mr Benson ran down the orchard.
'What's going on? You've got my
gun!'

Norman wasn't far behind. I
turned to them in a daze.

'I've shot the German.'

Norman ran over to Franz. 'He's dead. He's got our axe. It was him who took it. You got him just in time!'

Mr Benson put his hand on my shoulder. 'You brave lad. You got the swine.'

They led me back to the house, but I said nothing.

I was called a hero in the village. Stories went round about an evil German running at me with an axe. I'd shot him dead before he could raid the village. I knew it was nothing like that. I knew I'd done wrong and it was all a tragic mistake. The gun wasn't meant to go off.

I kept thinking of Julia. But I never saw her again. How was I to know they were in love? Nobody told us about sex in those days.

I was so upset and my mother came to take me home. I was pleased to leave the Bensons, but I never said goodbye to Julia.

Franz was a really good person. He didn't deserve what I did to him.

I never returned to the village.

The pain of what I did was too much.

The nightmares never stopped. Every night I saw Julia's face and heard her sobs. Night after night, year after year. The flashbacks struck ever since.

One night when I couldn't sleep, I saw a website. It was about the 75th anniversary of the start of the war and the village I once knew. A garden was being opened in memory of Mr Green, his wife and two children. I was stunned. That's when I knew I had to return.

TEN

I took a small box to the village.
I wanted to bury it there. Inside was
the letter Franz had given me to
look after. So was his watch and
ring. I'd never carried out his wishes.

Maybe that's why the nightmares never stopped.

I asked someone at the church about Mr Green.

'His grave is just there. He lived to a good age and is buried with his wife and daughter. His son was shot down in the war.'

'When did Julia die?' I asked.

'In the war – giving birth to little Frank. He still lives at the schoolhouse. He's made a garden there in their memory.'

I stood for a long time by a headstone with fading letters:

JULIA GREEN 1923 – 1942
A dear daughter and mother

I put flowers on the grave and told Julia the things I should have said years before. Then I walked across a field to where my den once stood. The orchard had gone, apart from one old pear tree. Tears filled my eyes as I spoke to Franz again.

I needed to see the schoolhouse. It was where I planned to bury my box … secretly in the garden.

I stood at the gate. It was where I first met Julia all those years ago.

'Can I help you?'

I stared at a man at the door.
Grey eyes looked down at me. It was
as if Franz himself had opened the
door.

'My name is Bernard,' I said.

The man smiled. 'Come in. We
always thought you'd come back.
My grandfather told me about you.
I'm Frank Green and my mother was
Julia. She died when I was born,
over 70 years ago.'

'I'm sorry … '

'You mustn't be sorry. Without
you, I wouldn't be here! My
grandfather brought me up and told
me about you. He and my mother

thought the world of you. Please come in and talk. I never knew my parents and you're the only person who knew them both.'

I told him my story. His eyes lit up. 'Thank you so much for telling me this. I knew nothing about my dad. I've never seen a picture of him.'

'I may have one,' I said. I took out my old box camera. 'The film is still inside. I guess it won't be any good now.'

Frank's face beamed. 'Let me try. I've got all the kit to develop photos upstairs. I do photography. This is amazing!'

I gave him Franz's watch, ring and the letter.

'At last I have an address in Germany. I never knew where he came from, so I couldn't trace his family. Now I can start!'

We went to his darkroom with the roll of film from my old camera. Under a dim red light, Frank began to work his magic. Very slowly we saw faces appear on paper in front of us. They were the smiling faces of the young lovers from 1941.

Frank was in tears. He put his arm round me.

'Thank you for coming back.

These photos are just what I need. I'm sorry if they're sad flashbacks for you.'

'I don't do flashbacks anymore,' I smiled. 'It's different now.'

It was true. Ghosts of the past had come home to rest. It was over.

No more nightmares. No more flashbacks. Peace at last.